MALTA
AN ARCHAEOLOGICAL PARADISE

Text
ANTHONY BONANNO

Design
JOSEPH BARTOLO

Photography
MARIO MINTOFF

Rear view of Ħaġar Qim main complex (background) from inside the north complex (foreground).

Photographs were taken by the courtesy of the Museums Department,
Valletta and the Cathedral Museum, Mdina.

Unless otherwise specified all illustrated archaeological items are at the
National Museum of Archaeology. Valletta.

Third edition 1991
Fourth edition 1993
Fifth edition 1995
Sixth edition 1996
New, update edition 1997

Photoset and printed in Malta by Interprint Limited

Front cover: Facade with the main entrance of Ħaġar Qim Temple complex.

Map of Malta and Gozo showing towns and villages (in italics), the main archaeological sites (in capitals) and other sites for the keener visitor.

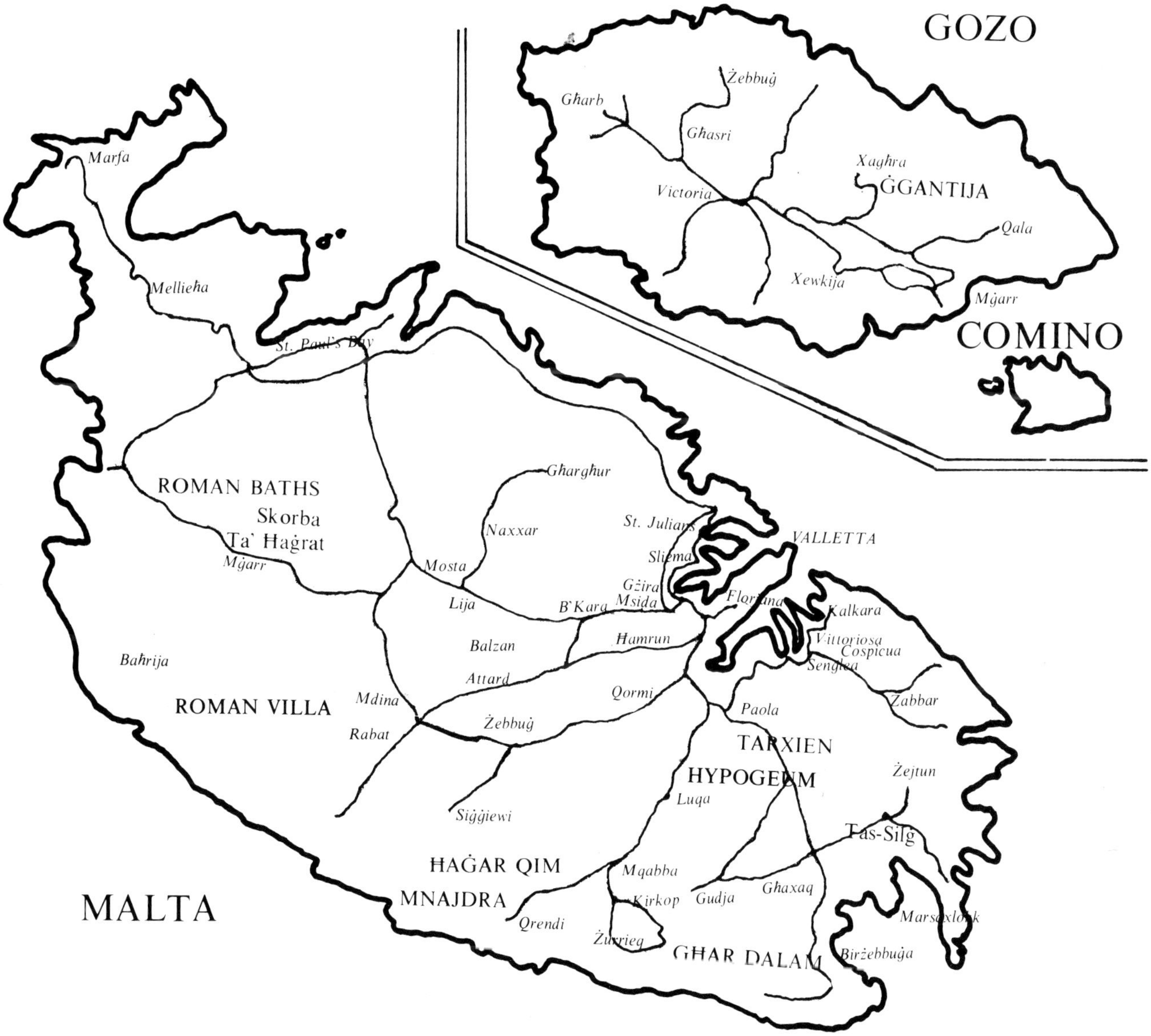

ITALY

SICILY
MALTA
GREECE

NORTH AFRICA

GOZO

Gharb
Żebbuġ
Ghasri
Xaghra
ĠGANTIJA
Victoria
Qala
Xewkija
Mġarr

COMINO

Marfa

Mellieha

St. Paul's Bay

ROMAN BATHS
Skorba
Ta` Ħaġrat
Mġarr

Gharghur

Naxxar

St. Julians

VALLETTA

Sliema

Mosta

Gżira
Msida
Floriana
Kalkara

Lija

B'Kara

Bahrija

Balzan

Ħamrun

Vittoriosa
Cospicua
Senglea

ROMAN VILLA
Mdina
Rabat

Attard

Qormi

Zabbar

Żebbuġ

Paola

TARXIEN

HYPOGEUM

Żejtun

Luqa

Siġġiewi

Tas-Silġ

ĦAĠAR QIM
MNAJDRA

Mqabba
Kirkop
Gudja
Ghaxaq

Qrendi

MALTA

Żurrieq

GĦAR DALAM

Marsaxlokk

Birżebbuġa

3

PREHISTORY

The story of man on the Maltese islands starts around 7000 years ago when the first humans crossed from nearby Sicily and settled here. Before that the islands were uninhabited by men. Various kinds of undomesticated animals, that denote a very different environment from the present one, dwelled unperturbed in them. Between 12,000 and 10,000 years ago, at the beginning of the Holocene, when the islands were detached for good from the continent, they were inhabited by red deer, bear, and most probably fox and wolf. Before that, probably during the Great Interglacial (around 250,000 years ago) considerable numbers of various species of dwarf elephants and hippopotami found themselves entrapped in this southernmost portion of the continental shelf that, due to the lowering of sea levels, extended from Malta to Sicily and joined the latter to the European mainland. Bones of these Pleistocene animals have been found in caves and crevices in several localities in Malta, but they were discovered in extraordinarily great quantities inside the cave called Għar Dalam, near Birżebbuġa.

Table showing the chronological sequence of Maltese archaeology from the earliest presence of man on the island down to the end of the Roman period.

PERIODS	PHASES	SUGGESTED CALIBRATED RADIOCARBON DATES B.C. (Renfrew 1972)	OTHER APPROXIMATE DATES B.C.
ROMAN			218 B.C.–A.D.535
PHOENICIO–PUNIC	Punic		550–218
	Phoenician		700–550
BRONZE (and IRON) AGE	Baħrija		900–700
	Borġ in-Nadur		1500–700
	Tarxien Cemetery	2500–1500	
TEMPLE PERIOD	Tarxien	3300 3000–2500	
	Saflieni		3300–3000
	Ġgantija	3600–3300 3000	
	Mġarr	3800–3600	
	Żebbuġ	4100–3800	
NEOLITHIC	Red Skorba	4400–4100	
	Grey Skorba	4500–4400	
	Għar Dalam	5000–4500	

Għar Dalam cave, near Birżebbuġa. Produced by an underground water stream in early geological times, this long gallery was occupied by man since his earliest settlement on the island (c. 5000 B.C.) down to the time of the first excavations in the 19th century.

◁

THE NEOLITHIC FARMERS

The Neolithic period unfurled itself through three cultural phases which succeeded each other without any apparent interruptions: the *Ghar Dalam, Grey Skorba* and *Red Skorba* phases.

The motivation behind the first crossing of men from Sicily to Malta is likely to remain a mystery, but we know that by that time, around 5000 B.C., southern Sicily was studded with farming communities whose needs for arable land became more and more pressing. Defensive works around villages of the Stentinello culture are indicative of tensions which might have prompted prospecting for new land. Now Malta must have been, as it still is, visible from the high grounds in the Ragusa region of southeast Sicily. It is probable that on a fine, clear day with a favourable north wind a scouting team was sent on a reliable sea-craft to explore this strange land on the southern horizon. They must have returned with news of a group of small but habitable islands. We can only imagine how, as a result of that exploratory expedition, several families set out to brave the ninety odd kilometres of open sea with the determination to start a new life on this new land. Their means of transport must have been even more sea-worthy, for they had to carry with them provisions of cereals and the first specimens of domestic lifestock in order to transfer their agricultural economy to their adoptive islands. It is likely that this operation was not carried out all at once, but in successive stages.

These early settlers brought also with them a characteristic pottery, known as *Impressed Ware*, with very close parallels to that of the *Stentinello* culture in southeast Sicily, although closer parallels have in recent years been claimed with pottery from Monte Kronio, a site near Agrigento. *Impressed Ware*, the characteristic pottery of the *Ghar Dalam* phase (c. 5000–4500 B.C.), derives its name from the geometric patterns impressed or incised on its surface before firing. Some decorations are produced by impressions made by the rippled edge of sea-shells, others by series of jabs with the finger-nails or a pointed stick or bone. Pottery found in a cave at Il-Mixta, Gozo, belongs to this phase, although some claim that it is of an even purer *Stentinello* pedigree than other *Ghar Dalam* pottery.

Throughout the nine to ten centuries of the Neolithic age, commercial and cultural contacts with the mother island were maintained: flint was imported to provide efficient cutting and pointed tools; obsidian, a superior raw material for the same purpose, originated in the rich volcanic

Ghar Dalam phase. Head of a horned animal (sheep or cattle) modelled in clay, probably a handle, from Għar Dalam. H. 0.06m.

deposits of Lipari and Pantelleria, reaching Malta most probably *via* Sicily; ideas for new fashions in pottery making continued to flow from the same direction. One would normally expect that some local product – one does not know exactly what – must have moved in the opposite direction.

Soon the new arrivals adapted themselves to the Maltese environment. For habitation they made use of the numerous caves and rocky shelters that abound in the Maltese limestone landscape. Ample evidence of such use was discovered, for example, at Għar Dalam which gives its name to the first phase of Maltese prehistory. But they also converged in small villages consisting of groups of huts built of wattle-and-daub (or mud-brick) on very low stone foundations. The only settlement of this type to be properly investigated so far is that of Skorba, a site near Mġarr (Malta), after which the *Grey Skorba* and *Red Skorba* phases (c. 4500–4100 B.C.) are named.

During the *Grey Skorba* phase the *Għar Dalam* pottery is replaced by a rather dull, undecorated ware of greyish colour. Eventually the same fabric is given a bright red coating – hence *Red Skorba* – but the shapes continue to be more or less the same. This red slip, as well as a very characteristic ladle with a horn-shaped handle, and the equally characteristic 'trumpet-lugs', all have close parallels in the pottery of the contemporary *Diana* culture of the Lipari islands and Sicily.

Besides evidence of the way of life, economy and commercial contacts of the earliest Maltese inhabitants, we are lucky to be in possession of material relics that throw light also on their religious beliefs. At Skorba two huts, of a larger size than normal, seem to have been used as shrines. In one of them, fragments of several female figurines were found, with pronounced sexual attributes. They have been connected with the worship of a 'Mother Goddess' or 'Goddess of Fertility' that promoted the productivity of the land.

Prehistoric tool kit of different phases, from Għar Dalam. Various instruments, including blades, points and scrapers in obsidian, flint, local chert, and bone. Also, two examples of biconical slingstones in local limestone. The flint core in the centre is flanked by two miniature axes in hard green stone, probably personal ornaments (pendants).

Modern reconstructed model of a nude figure with unmistakable female sexual attributes. The original figurines, in clay and stone, have survived in a fragmentary state. The context in which they were found suggests a religious meaning, perhaps a "Mother Goddess". A number of features bear close resemblance to figurines from the Cyclades. From Skorba. H. c.0.08m.

Biconical vase with the characteristic red slip and trumpet-shaped handles of the *Red Skorba* phase. The handles are set vertically just below the rim and are perforated, probably for hanging by means of a string. From Skorba. H. c.0.15m.

Distinctive *Red Skorba* clay ladle with horn-shaped handle. Note the wear on the lip which suggests use for drinking. From Skorba. H. 0.15m.

Jar of unknown provenance with typical clay and incised decoration of the *Żebbuġ* phase. Incised pattern is suggestive of the human form. H. 0.152m.

THE TEMPLE BUILDERS

The second age of Maltese prehistory takes its name from the extraordinary stone structures which characterize it and which, as has been suggested, should be included among the seven wonders of the prehistoric world. It is preferable not to call this period 'Copper Age' because that term would denote a technological innovation within it for which we have absolutely no evidence.

ŻEBBUĠ

The first phase, *Żebbuġ* (c. 4100–3800 B.C.), marks the arrival in Malta of a new group of farmers, again from Sicily, with connections with the *San Cono-Piano Notaro* cultures there. Their ceramic kit is markedly different from that of the preceding phase – hence the suggestion of a new immigrant wave – but the rest of their material culture, as well as their commercial contacts overseas, remain essentially the same. The type-site produced a group of collective rock-cut tombs from which highly characteristic pear-shaped jars and a heavily stylized anthropomorphic head were retrieved. Unfortunately, the rest of the body of the latter is missing, but it bears striking similarities to the statue-menhirs of southern France and Sardinia. It is also quite enigmatic because it does not seem to be related in any way either to the previous anthropomorphic figurines of *Red Skorba*, or to the later, more emphatic, expressions of the human form peculiar to the temple culture. Other highly schematized human representations occur in the pottery decoration which is either painted or incised.

Complete pear-shaped jar of the *Żebbuġ* phase with two large handles on shoulders and two smaller ones on neck at right angles to them. Typical incised decoration, mostly curvilinear. A series of triangular jabs above and below line of separation between neck and shoulders. Unknown provenance. H. 0.165m.

So-called "statue-menhir" from its close resemblance to statue-menhirs from southern France. Head of an extremely stylized anthropomorphic figure, broken at the shoulders. Perhaps a divinity connected with death, or an ancestral image. Globigerina limestone with traces of red ochre. From the Ta' Trapna rock-cut tombs, near Żebbuġ. H. 0.195m.

A Limestone miniature model of a simple temple unit of oval shape. It strongly suggests that temples were actually roofed over. From Ta' Ħaġrat, Mġarr. H. 0.045m.

B Bowl handle with end in the shape of a ram's head. From Ta' Ħaġrat, Mġarr. Max. H. 0.08m.

C View of the trilithic entrance of the western, trefoil-shaped temple at Ta' Ħaġrat, Mġarr.

C

MĠARR

The following phase, *Mġarr* (c. 3800–3600 B.C.), is no more than a short transitional stage, as one can see from the typical pottery. The decoration, consisting of mostly curved lines, is produced by means of cut-out bands.

13

ĠGANTIJA

The Xemxija collective rock-cut tombs span this phase and the next one, *Ġgantija* (c. 3600–3000 B.C.). It is during the latter phase that the temples make their first appearance, either as a reproduction above ground of the underground lobed tombs or, possibly, a more durable version in stone of flimsier structures that have not survived. Modest and simple at first, they become more and more imposing and intricate. Within the Ġgantija phase itself the internal plan of the temples evolves from the trefoil to the symmetrical five-apsed plan.

The type-site, Gozo's precious gift to the world, is a truly *megalithic* complex (in the Greek sense of the word) consisting of two temple units of the five-apsed plan with a common outer wall but separate entrances. The building is still impressive by its sheer size, the gargantuan dimensions of some of its stone blocks and the surprisingly good state of preservation.

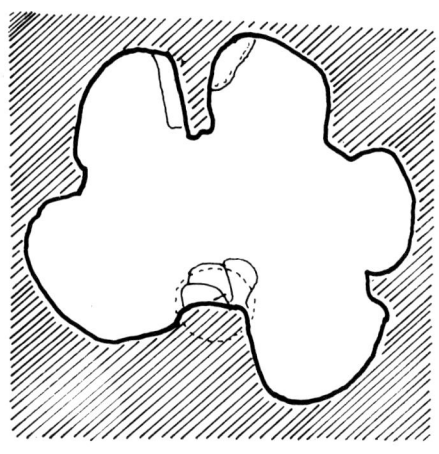 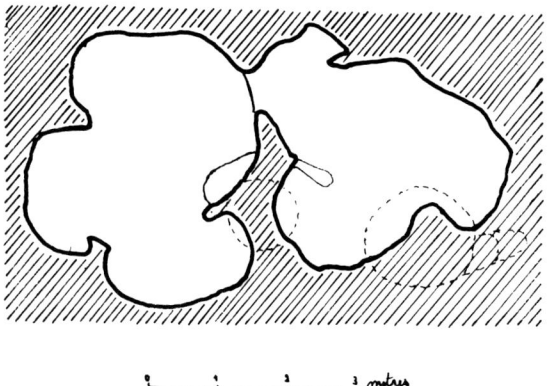

Plans of Tomb 5 (left) and Tombs 1 and 2 (right) at Xemxija. These are collective tombs and seem to be the predecessors of the much more complex Ħal Saflieni collective cemetery. According to one widely-accepted theory, their shape inspired the original lobed plan of the earliest temples, a plan which evolved rapidly into the 'trefoil' plan.

Plan of trefoil temple at Mnajdra. From the trefoil plan to that with five apses of the South Temple at Ġgantija the change was a remarkably small one and required only the addition of a further pair of apses.

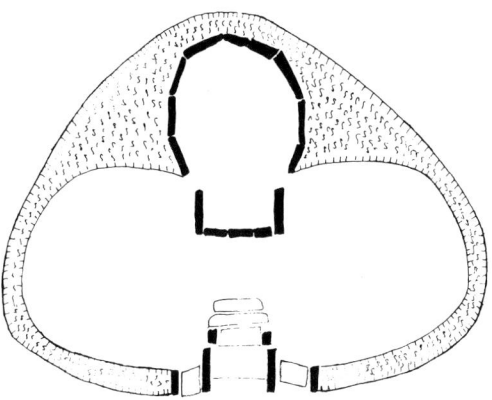

Plan of the Ġgantija complex showing a common outer wall enclosing two temple units, one with five apses and the other with four apses and a niche at the far end.

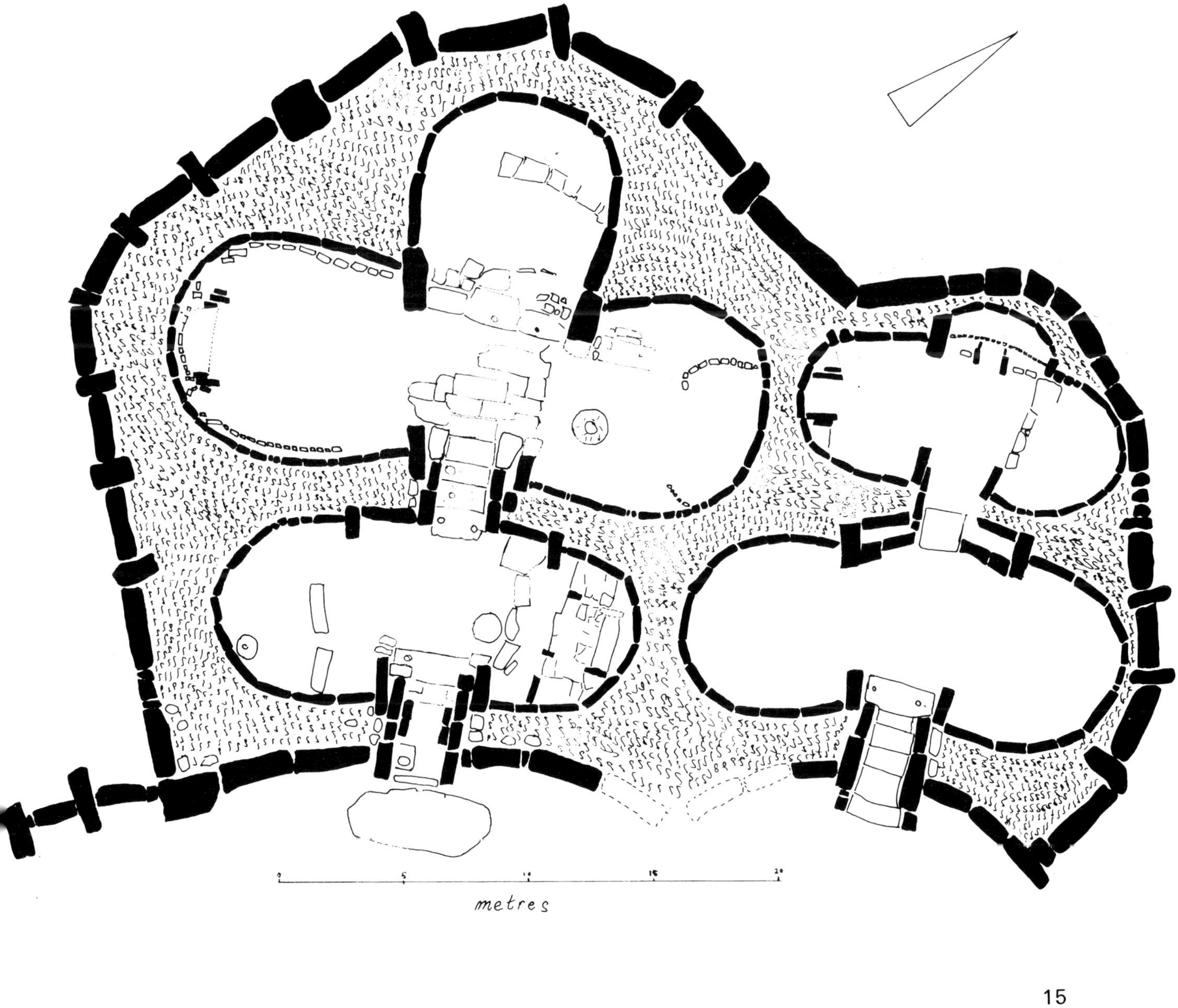

metres

South Temple at Ġgantija. View of the paved central passageway and the apse with three trilithic niches, from the opposite end.

Ġgantija Temples. View of the paved passageway and entrance of the South Temple from the back. Note the rough-shaped blocks in hard coralline limestone of the walls in contrast with the well-finished smooth surfaces of the blocks in Globigerina limestone flanking the passageways.

Cast of one of two heads in Globigerina limestone found at Ġgantija. It has puffed cheeks and wears a wig-like headdress or hairstyle. The flat base of the neck suggests that the head is complete. H. 0.17m.

Partly restored deep bowl with a single handle and a small knob on the opposite side. Curvilinear scratched decoration closely resembling the 'comet' motif typical of Ġgantija ware. From Għar ta' Għejżu, near Ġgantija. H. 0.09m.

Aerial view of the Ġgantija complex from the back.

THE HYPOGEUM

Another short transitional phase, *Saflieni* (c. 3300–3000 B.C.), takes its name from the place-name of the Hypogeum, that unique structure hewn out of the living rock in three successive storeys. Unfortunately, its interpretation is still shrouded in mystery due to the primitive method by which it was excavated immediately after its discovery in 1902, and it is the dream of many, archaeologists most of all, to discover another such structure in order to be able to throw surer, more objective, light on the purpose and function of its individual features. One would like to know, for example, the real purpose of the so-called 'Holy of Holies' and of the entire lower storey. Are we right in interpreting one of the chambers as the 'Oracle Room'? Meanwhile we can only guess, and one guess is as good as another. What we can say for certain is that the Hypogeum had two purposes. It was mainly a place of burial where the remains of several thousand individuals were deposited in some state or other along with personal ornaments and pottery items. But it must have also been a place of worship with architectural features resembling closely those of the temples above ground. The cult of the dead (or of the ancestors) seems here to be intimately linked with that of the Mother Earth. It may well be that these people believed that their entry into the bowels of the earth for certain religious rites symbolized a temporary return to the womb of Mother Earth from which all life derived and to which they were destined to return definitely at death.

Modern plastic model of the Hypogeum at Ħal Saflieni. In the foreground is the modern spiral staircase. The original entrance, preceded by a me-galithic structure, appears in the top right corner.

The Hypogeum. Large hall with architectural features, like trilithons and blind niches, in imitation of the temples above ground.

Two figurines from the Hypogeum. The so-called 'Sleeping Lady', representing a woman with abundant forms lying on her right side on a couch. It may suggest the practice of the rite of incubation. L. 0.12m. Headless standing alabaster statuette of an extremely fat human figure with no clear indication of its sex. H. 0.062m.

The Hypogeum. Three-quarter view of the façade of the 'Holy of Holies' at the far end of the middle floor. Note the faithful imitation of the architectural features of the temples above ground, including the corbelling of the walls.

A

B

Pottery items from the Hypogeum.

A Cover with modern-looking, abstract decoration: a polished radial design against a pitted background. Diam. 0.19m.

B Another cover with a design vaguely suggesting the human form against a similar background. Diam. 0.15m.

C Large carinated bowl in fine, hard-fired and well-polished ware with scratched curvilinear decoration. Diam. 0.39m.

The Hypogeum. Section of the intricate spiral design in red ochre on the walls and ceiling of the 'Oracle Room'.

Reconstructed necklace made up of pierced shell discs and beads and one axe-shaped pendant in light-grey stone. Such personal ornaments were buried with the dead.

Seemingly female limestone head. It fits well in the head socket of a headless standing statuette of the usual fat type found in the same room of the Hypogeum. H. 0.11m.

ĦAĠAR QIM AND MNAJDRA TEMPLES

Tarxien phase (c. 3000–2500 B.C.) constitutes the climax of the temple 'civilization'. Several temple complexes were erected during this phase, such as, Ħaġar Qim, Mnajdra, Borġ in-Nadur and Tas-Silġ. Ħaġar Qim offers a spectacular sight not only for the gigantic size of many of its stone blocks, but also for its neatly designed and carefully assembled facade which reproduces in real dimensions the lower part of a model of a temple facade found at Tarxien.

Excavated at the beginning of the nineteenth century, Ħaġar Qim has produced as many as seven 'fat figure' statuettes, the more naturalistic nude 'Venus of Malta', and the unparalleled four-sided altar with a stylized representation of a potted plant on each side. An open-air shrine inserted into the outer wall on the north flank of the facade seems to combine in a very suggestive way the symbols of the male and female generative organs. Ħaġar Qim also preserves a small section of corbelling or oversailing walls illustrating the construction technique used to narrow the span of the roof, the same technique that was employed more than a thousand years later in the *tholoi* of Mycenae. Even better preserved sections of corbelling can be examined in the Mnajdra complex just a kilometre downhill from Ħaġar Qim. Here we seem to have the only ascertainable 'astronomical' alignment. The overall majority of temple units face southwards, that is any direction south of east or south of west. But the south unit of the Mnajdra complex is perfectly aligned with the rising sun at the equinoxes. As the equinox sunrise is extremely difficult to determine, however, scientists have serious doubts as to whether this alignment was intentional.

The Tas-Silġ temple is the last to be discovered, having been brought to light by an Italian archaeological mission in 1963. It is quite unusual in consisting of one single unit with entrances at both ends of the main axis, and in retaining its religious function in successive ages. The same temple was extended in Phoenician times, and on the same site Punic, Roman and Byzantine religious buildings were erected. Ironically enough Tas-Silġ is not very far from the Borġ in-Nadur temple, one of the two groups of prehistoric ruins to be mentioned for the first time in modern literature, namely, in the *Insulae Melitae Descriptio* published by the Frenchman Jean Quintin in 1536.

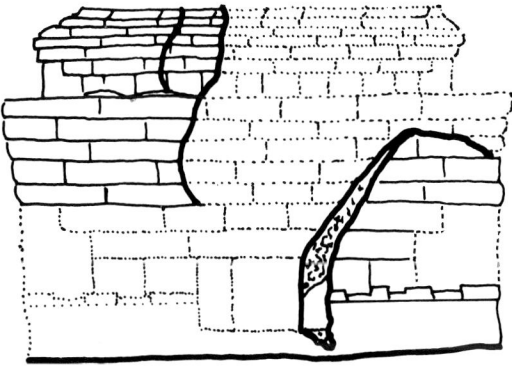

Model of a temple facade reconstructed from four original fragments from Tarxien Temples. To be compared with the facade of the main complex at Ħaġar Qim (following page).

23

Plan of the main temple complex of Ḥaġar Qim.

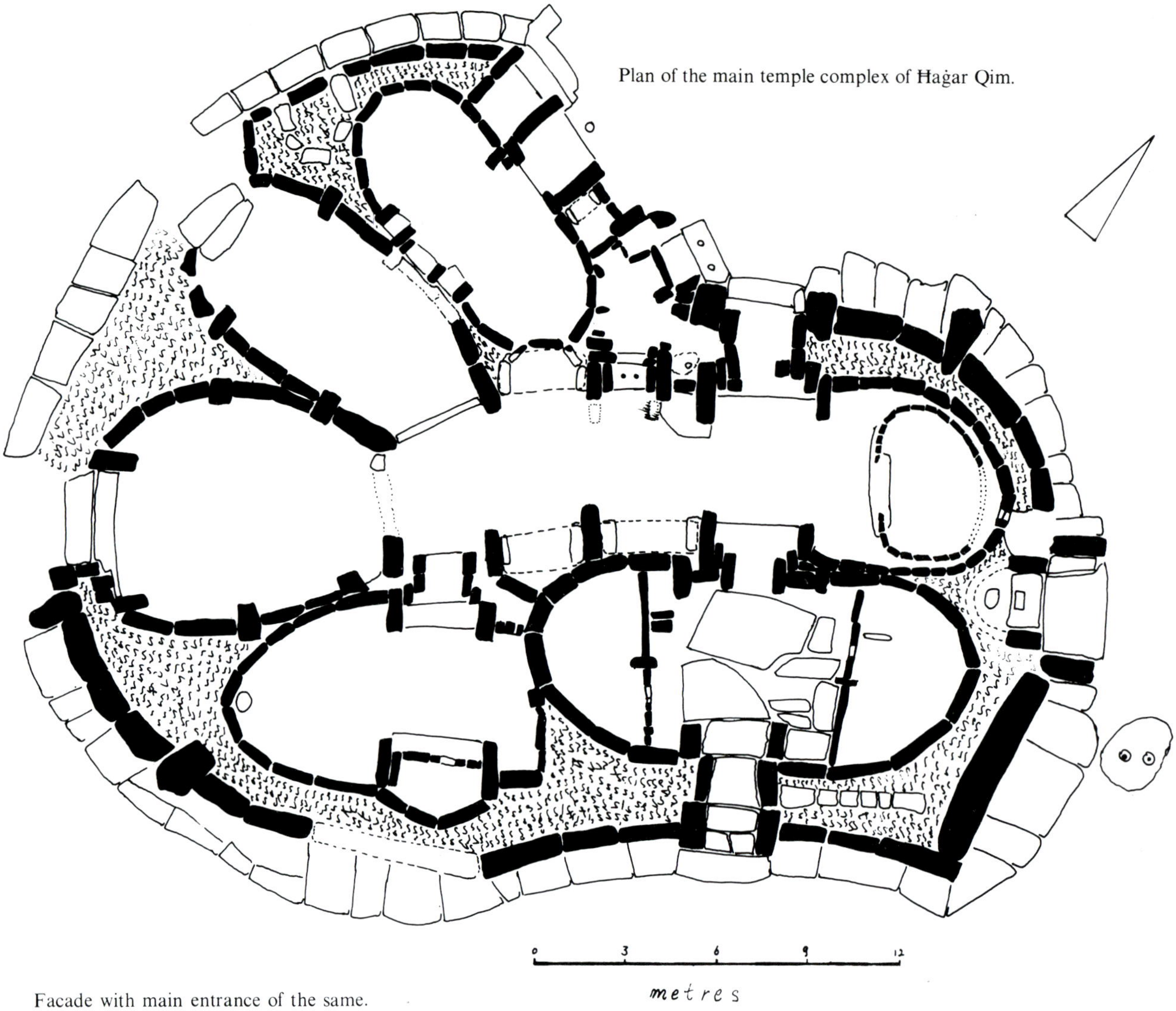

Facade with main entrance of the same.

0   3   6   9   12

m e t r e s

The so-called 'Venus of Malta'. Headless clay figurine representing a standing nude woman with naturalistic, albeit somewhat opulent, features. From Ħaġar Qim. Max. H. 0.13m.

C

Ħaġar Qim, main temple complex.

A Passageway flanked by two pedestalled, or mushroom-shaped, altars.

B Shrine inserted into the outer wall. In the centre an isolated betyl preceded by a triangular slab, suggestive of the human generative organs (?).

C Second apse on the right showing the clearly converging walls to reduce the roof span.

Four-sided limestone altar. Each side shows in low relief a plant growing from a pot and flanked by two projecting pilasters. The surfaces are decorated with round drilled pittings. From Ḥaġar Qim. H. 0.73m.

Two of several limestone statuettes found in Ħaġar Qim. Squatting stylized figures with extremely obese features but no sexual attributes. One preserves a hollow socket for insertion of a separately worked head. H. 0.235 and 0.21m.

A

Three views of the Mnajdra Temples.

A Middle Temple. Porthole slab encased within trilithon.

B Lower Temple. The best example of corbelling walls.

C The whole complex against the sea. Islet of Filfla in the distance.

B

C

Plan of the Lower and Middle Temples at Mnajdra, both constructed during the *Tarxien* phase.

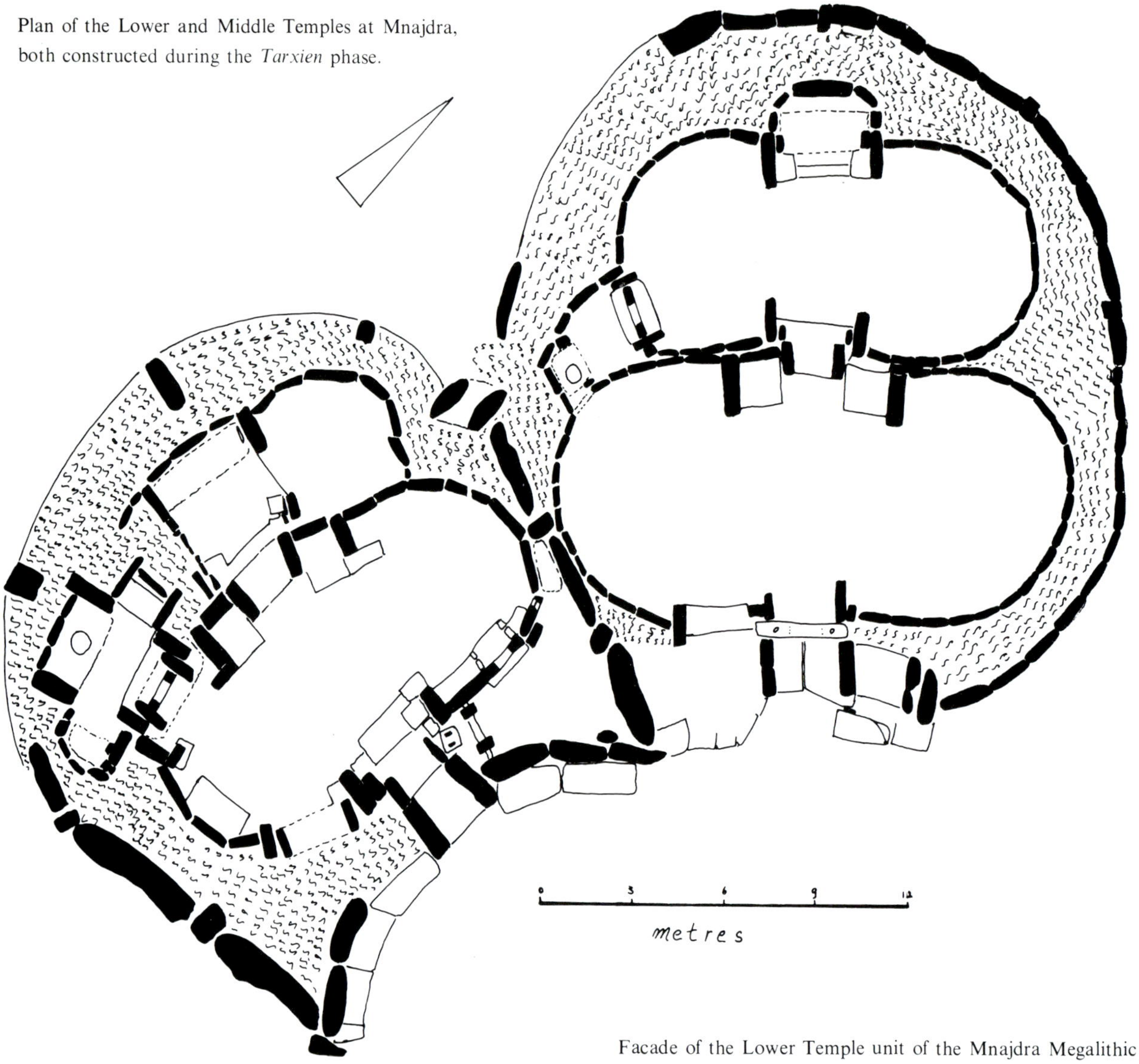

metres

Facade of the Lower Temple unit of the Mnajdra Megalithic comple

Lower Temple. View of elaborately designed shrine consisting of a port-hole slab within a trilithon preceded by two trapezoidal slabs. The whole facade is covered with pittings.

Altar block with two symmetrical spirals in relief. From the Buġibba Temple. L. 1.08m.

View of the few remains that survive of the Buġibba Temple.

Altar block with three fishes carved in very low relief. From Buġibba. It has been suggested that the species represented is the *Sargus rondeleti* which is commonly found in Maltese waters. L. 0.94m.

TARXIEN TEMPLES

The temple complex that gave its name to this last phase of the temple period is that of Tarxien, situated only a few hundred metres away from the Hypogeum. This proximity of the two monuments suggests some special relation between the two, perhaps a control over the latter by the priesthood of the former. The Tarxien temples turned out to be the richest deposit of prehistoric art objects on the islands, left untouched for thousands of years until they were brought to light again during the years of World War I. Most of these can be enjoyed at the National Museum of Archaeology in Valletta. Copies of the removed stone sculptures have been placed instead of them, and some original pottery items are still housed in the small antiquarium annexed to the site. The erosion on the copies *in situ* reveals how wise it was to have the originals moved indoors and replaced by copies.

There are four distinct temple units at Tarxien. The earliest one, of smaller size and quite separate from the others, was built in the Ġgantija phase and has the typical five-apsed plan. The other three are joined together by a common outer wall. The last unit to be erected is the middle one which was wedged in between the other two, thus spoiling much of their symmetry. It is the only example of the most advanced temple plan, that with three pairs of apses symmetrically disposed along the long axis that conducted the visitor from the entrance to the niche at the back end. Even architecturally it marks the most refined achievement both aesthetically and technically. There are some architectonic features in one of the small semicircular chambers which suggest that these people had come to grips with the principle of the vertical arch and of the dome structure.

Equally astonishing for a prehistoric society, still lacking the sophisticated heirarchical structure typical of the 'civilizations' of the eastern Mediterranean, is the temple people's achievement in the field of sculpture and ceramic art. We have already referred to the mysterious sculptures of fat figures examples of which were discovered at Ħaġar Qim. A statue of the same type but of colossal size – originally it must have stood more than two metres high – was the centre-piece among several other pieces of sculpture, in relief, that adorned the vestibule of the Tarxien complex. If size is a valid criterion to determine whether a divinity or a human being is represented, then there is very little doubt that this is a divine figure. The relief sculpture in front and on either side of the statue offers an array of pleasant variations on the same theme, the spiral. It too must have had a special meaning, a meaning which we can only attempt to decipher but can never be sure of. The rows of animals carved in relief on two slabs found in the same area contrast their very naturalistic message with the abstract one of the spirals.

Spirals and volutes are just two varieties of decoration adopted to embellish the pottery. These patterns are normally incised on the polished surface of the pot, but sometimes they are formed by applied small discs or against a stippled background. Some large containers are given a rusticated or 'scaly' surface. To my mind, however, the most gratifying factor of the pottery of this age is the wide range of shapes which, though hand-made, reach such a perfection as to be comparable with those of Classical Greece. All this, it should be remembered, was achieved without apparent foreign inspiration.

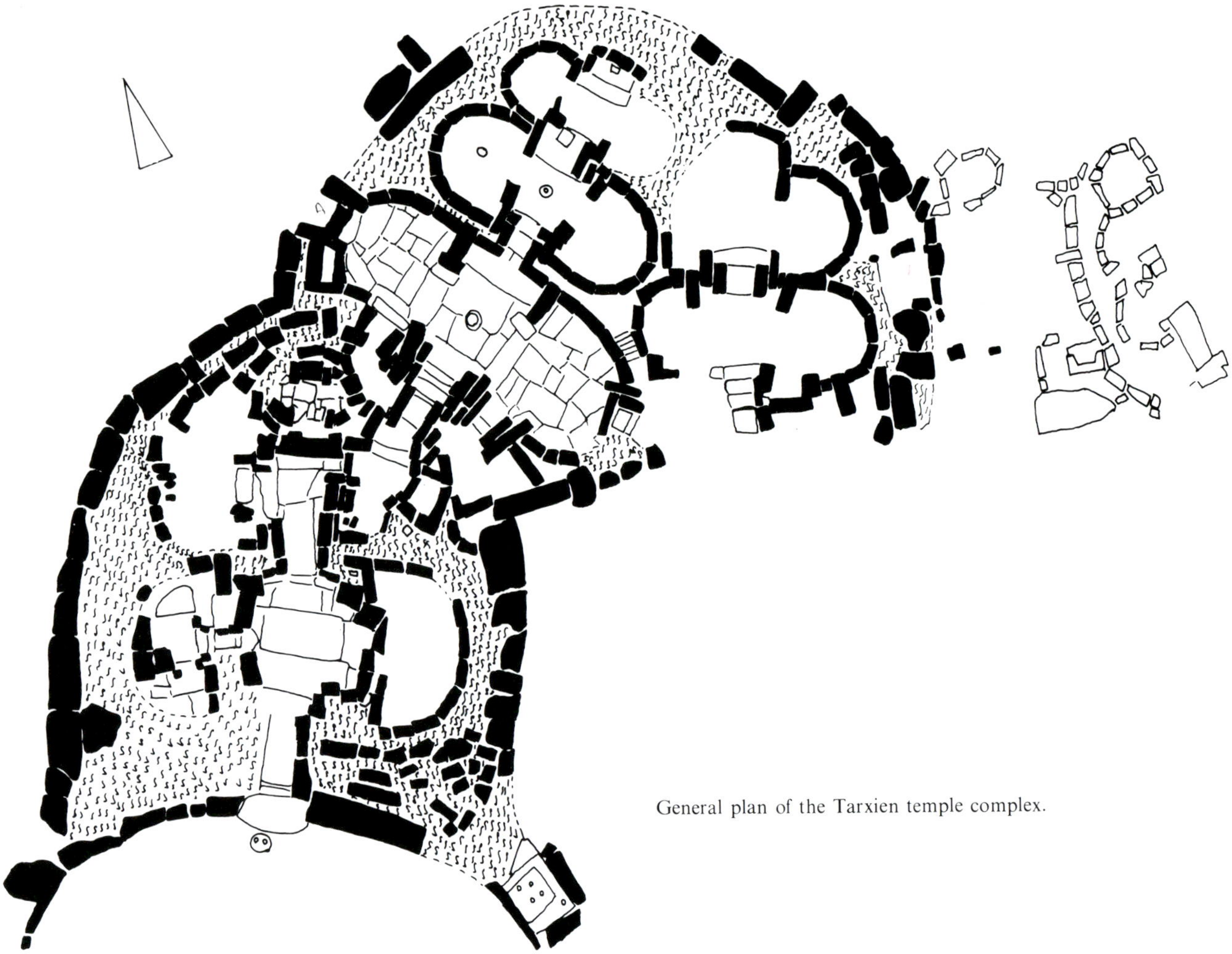

General plan of the Tarxien temple complex.

View of the inner niche of the South Temple.
A raised threshold carved with an elaborate
system of spirals seems to inhibit access to
the innermost part of the temple.

View of the first apse on the right in the South Temple, once dominated by a colossal statue of the usual obese type of which only the lower half survives. When whole the statue must have stood about 2m. in height. The originals of the statue and of the relief decoration are in the Museum of Archaeology, Valletta.

A fragmentary carved limestone slab showing two phalli enclosed in a niche. Traces of red ochre on pitted base and on phalli. H. 0.115m.

Huge basin in first left apse of Middle Temple. Now restored from several pieces, originally it was hewn from a single block of stone. H. c. 1m.

Animal figures carved in relief on wall slabs of small room tucked between South and Middle Temples. The top figure clearly represents a horned bull. The small figure below it is commonly interpreted as a sow suckling thirteen piglets. Fertility symbolism again?

Narrow frieze showing a procession of different animals: four sheep or goats, a pig and, probably, a ram. Sacrificial victims?

Another narrow frieze showing two rows of sheep or goats.

One of two large screens in Globigerina limestone that used to flank the inner side of the trilithic passageway into the second pair of apses of the Middle Temple at Tarxien. The screen is decorated with four symmetrically disposed spirals in low relief against a pitted background. The originals are at the National Museum in Valletta having been replaced by faithful copies on the site. H. c.1.40m.

Pottery of various shapes and types of decoration.

A Large, roughly biconical vase with narrow neck and two large tunnel handles. Well fired clay with polished surface. H. 0.41m.

B Large, roughly biconical vase with wide neck and no handles. Scale-like decoration on the lower part. H. 0.35m.

C Carinated bowl with high handle. Intricate design of wavy lines on outer surface of lower part of handle. Total H. 0.175m.

D Two carinated bowls decorated with studs placed closely against a background covered with white paste. Volute pattern on lower portion. H. left: 0.155m., right: 0.09m.

Hollow terracotta statuette representing a standing figure, probably male, wearing a pleated skirt. The hieratic pose and wig-like hair-style, as well as the difference in style and concept from the usual 'fat' figures, suggest a representation of a priest. Portrait-like features. Original H. 0.60m.

Left apse at the rear end of the Middle Temple at Tarxien. Remarkable is the perfect fit between the upright slabs. Above them the only surviving block of the first horizontal course has an inclined upper surface suggesting the spring of an arched dome. Could it be that by the end of the Temple period this culture had come to grips with the arch principle? Several prehistorians have expressed serious doubts on this possibility.

XAGHRA STONE CIRCLE

What has been observed above about the special relationship between the Tarxien temples and the Ħal Saflieni Hypogeum can also be applied to the spatial connection between the Ġgantija temples and the Xagħra Stone Circle, an underground cemetery that has been explored and excavated since the publication of the first edition of this work. This collective cemetery was set inside a subterranean system of natural caves, just below the surface of the hill top overlooking Ġgantija, some 300 metres to its west. The cemetery was at some stage monumentalised and secured by a circular boundary wall of large, standing and interlocking coralline stones with a monumental entrance on the east side, facing the Ġgantija temples. It was this circular wall which gave the site its name.

Unfortunately, the wall has all but disappeared; but a rich documentation survives from the late 18th and early 19th centuries, consisting of descriptions, engravings and watercolours, which illustrate it in its pristine condition. This documentation has permitted the identification of the site with a circular field south of the Gozitan town of Xagħra. The excavation of the site, conducted over a period of eight years by the Universities of Bristol, Cambridge and Malta and the Museums Department, confirmed this identification.

The most revealing illustrations are two watercolour views of the stone circle by the artist Charles de Brochtorff dating to about 1820: one from the east side, the other from the west showing the circle with the Ġgantija temples, Nuffara hill and Comino and Malta in the background. The latter also shows a huge hole in the centre of the circular field, inside which impressive megalithic structures appear below ground level. Moreover, a man is seen coming out of a cave with a human skull in his hand. The recent archaeological excavations have had to carefully distinguish the modern backfill of this 19th century hole from the uncontaminated prehistoric deposits.

The same excavations have also revealed that initially a small tomb had been dug in the *Żebbuġ* phase consisting of a vertical shaft serving two roughly circular chambers. More than sixty individuals were buried in succession in these chambers together with their personal ornaments, like bone and stone pendants. The bone amulets have roughly human shapes while the axe-shaped stone pendants must have been items of prestige, imported from overseas, some from as far as the Alps. The burial ritual must have involved the application of red ochre, since a large quantity of it was found strewn all over the place, particularly in one chamber. A stylised human bust of stone was placed at the entrance of one of the chambers, as if intended to guard the tomb. It is almost identical to the "statue-menhir" from the Ta' Trapna tombs near Żebbuġ, Malta (p. 12). The tombs were used only in the *Żebbuġ* phase, with a single intrusion during the *Ġgantija* phase.

It seems that at this stage the burial ritual was transferred to the pre-existing large cave system close by. Here the subterranean spaces were further separated and differentiated by the introduction of screens, trilithons and uprights carved from the softer globigerina limestone which had to be quarried some distance away from the site itself. The ritual ceremonies connected with the burial seem to have been held in a central area reached from the surface down a few steps. Here a large stone jar could have served some lustral purpose. Close to it, an unusual statue group was found face down, as if it had fallen from a higher level, probably a trilithic niche, on which it might have been placed to be seen by all. The group consists of two draped figures of the usual corpulent type, sitting side by side on an intricately worked couch. One figure holds a cup on its lap while the other holds a miniature version of itself,

Watercolour by Charles de Brochtorff showing the 1920 excavation inside the Xagħra Circle. The Ġgantija temples, Comino and Malta are visible in the background.

VIEW OF THE EXCAVATION, BEGUN NEAR, THE TWO LARGE STONE PILLARS

View of the underground cave system inside the Xagħra Circle during the 1987-1994 excavations. The roof of the caves had already collapsed in antiquity.

possibly a child. The statuette was originally coloured over with red, yellow and black. Traces of these colours have survived, mostly the red on the upper surface of the couch and on the legs.

A statue of the same obese figure type, but about one metre in height, must have stood somewhere in the same area. However, it must have been shattered purposely in small fragments and scattered all over the area. It wore the typical pleated skirts and was extremely finely finished. It too has preserved a few traces of yellow paint.

A more mysterious set of figurines were discovered packed tightly together, suggesting that originally they were kept in a bundle. They have no parallels anywhere, not even in the Maltese context. Six of them have human heads supported by plain triangular bodies without any limbs. Their size and shape make them ideal for grasping in the hand for some ritual or other. Three smaller figurines are even stranger. One human head is attached to a two-limbed animal body, and another tops a slightly convex, cylindrical stand on a flat, cone-shaped base, reminiscent of the human-headed phalli of the Classical age. The third one is a pig's head attached to a plain cylindrical stand.

What is even more intriguing about the plank-like figures is that while two of them are perfectly finished, the other four are in various stages of finish, their form gradually freeing itself from the stone.

Another class of anthropomorphic representations is represented by about a dozen terracotta figurines found scattered in another area to the west of the previous one. Some are intact while others have survived only in limited fragments. These have close parallels from the Hal Saflieni hypogeum and are characterised by their enormous buttocks and thighs and small torso and limbs.

In spite of this abundant figurative repertory produced by this new archaeological site, it might turn out that its greatest contribution is in another field, the human skeletal remains themselves. Literally hundreds of thousands of bone fragments have been patiently unearthed, examined and identified. For the moment it is estimated that they belonged to a minimum of one thousand individuals. This alone makes it the richest Neolithic collective cemetery discovered so far. The scientific potential of such a plentiful body of human bones is immense and its study by specialists is already in hand and has already produced the first results. The individuals buried in the Żebbuġ phase tombs, for example, appear to have belonged to an unusually healthy population. Those buried in the later, larger complex were perhaps less healthy, but not to a considerable degree. Their teeth tended to be surprisingly well preserved, in spite of the calculus.

Within the apparent confusion in the distribution of human bone remains in this underground cemetery, on closer examination of their respective findspots, one finds a certain patterning or clustering of bones, mostly based on age and gender, rather than on social differentiation. Thus, the central area around the large stone vase was taken up predominantly by female and children's skeletal remains, while the bone pit to the north of the paved threshold above it contained as many as eight layers of bones of mature male individuals. Again, although most of the human bone was found loosely scattered, or in partial articulation, suggesting that the site was an ossuary for secondary burial, rather than a proper cemetery, there was an appreciable number of completely articulated skeletons, almost invariably directly on the floor of the cave, or in specially dug pits. From the scanty records we have of the Hal Saflieni Hypogeum excavation it appears that the same was experienced there.

The most important difference is that in the Xaghra Circle case the excavation has been properly documented. There is no doubt that a deeper study of the patterns of distribution of bone remains in relation to the spatial context in which they were deposited, and the figurative and other material associated with them, will provide new insights in the religious beliefs and social interaction of this extraordinary human community.

ne of the dozen or so terracotta figurines found in the section west of the
entral area, inside the underground cemetery. Very peculiar are the
flated thighs and buttocks in contrast with the very flat upper torso. H.
.083m.

mall limestone stele with very stylized, incised, human facial features.
rom the entrance of one of the *Żebbuġ* phase tombs. H. 0.168m.

Two articulated skeletons, one placed over the other, found in a semi-
flexed position in the farthest corner of the eastern extension of the
underground cave.

An artist's impression of the Xagħra Circle as it might have been when it was in use as a communal burial in the *Tarxien* phase. (Drawing by Giovanni Caselli).

▲ A statuette with two corpulent figures wearing elaborate skirts and seated on a tiered couch. The left figure holds a smaller version of itself on her lap, while the right one holds a hollow cup. From the central area. H. 0.124m.

1-6: A set of six limestone figurines each having a plain, plank-like body surmounted by a human head. Average H. 0.17m. 7-9: smaller limestone figurines, two having human heads while the third has a pig's head. From the central area. Average H. 0.07m.

THE BRONZE AGE WARRIORS

Several explanations have been suggested for the mysterious disappearance of the temple people but none of them can be proved in an empirical way. However, over-exploitation and eventual exhaustion of the natural resources, compounded by successive years of drought which forced the entire population to desert the island, seems so far the most plausible solution to the enigma. What the archaeological record reveals unequivocally is that around 2500 B.C. a new people, carrying an entirely different culture, settled on and started to repopulate the islands which by that time seem to have been completely deserted. Contrary to the previous inhabitants, the new folk disposed of their dead by cremation and made use of bronze tools and weapons, both factors revealing their kinship with the Bronze Age warlike peoples occupying Greece, southern Italy and Sicily round about the same time.

The first phase of the Maltese Bronze Age, *Tarxien Cemetery* (c. 2500–1500 B.C.) is represented by a cremation cemetery, the only one known so far, that was inserted right in the midst of the ruins of the Tarxien temples. In a dark grey layer of ashy soil rows of open cinerary urns were found containing remains of cremated human bodies. Small flat beads were found in abundance, no doubt items of personal ornaments that accompanied the deceased to their final place of rest, as did other personal possessions, like the bronze axes and flat dagger blades. The urns often contained smaller pots as well as carbonized seeds and plant stems. Various lumps of textile fabrics may have been the remains of the clothing in which the deceased were incinerated. In the same layer Temi Zammit, the Maltese archaeologist who excavated the Tarxien complex, found also a group of highly stylized anthropomorphic terracotta figurines in a seated posture. Two of them are recognizably female whereas the body of the others is rendered as a flat disc covered with incised geometric patterns, one of which looking very much like an ancestor of the Maltese cross.

We still have no indication of the type of settlement used by the *Tarxien Cemetery* folk and the only architectural feature associated with them is the *dolmen*, various examples of which, of different sizes, are scattered in both islands. Referred to in Maltese toponymy as *l-imsaqqfa* ('the roofed one'), the *dolmen* is a single-room structure consisting of a horizontal, roughly shaped slab of stone supported on three sides by blocks of stone standing on end. Their purpose seems to have been a funerary one. They have parallels in the Otranto region in southeast Italy as well as in northwest Europe.

The evidence of insecurity and warfare becomes stronger in the second Bronze Age phase, *Borġ in-Nadur* (c. 1500–700 B.C.), which takes its name from the site of a fortified village in the Marsaxlokk area. The village consisted of a group of oval huts situated on a triangular promontory which was retained to be naturally defensible on the two steep sides, but had to be fortified by a massive wall in the 'Cyclopean' technique on the flatter side. Other *Borġ in-Nadur* villages have been identified both in Malta and Gozo: they tend to be sited on high flat-topped hills, such as Fawwara and Wardija ta' San

Ġorġ in Malta, and In-Nuffara in Gozo. Very typical of this phase are shallow bottle-shaped pits in the ground which seem to have been used for storage of either grain or water. Groups of these have been noted in places like Wardija ta' San Ġorġ, the Mtarfa promontory, In-Nuffara and Borġ in-Nadur itself. Close to the latter site a group of such pits are to be found right on the edge of the seashore – unfortunately much damaged in recent years. Some of them are actually submerged, thus indicating a considerable subsidence of this part of the island in the last three millennia.

Typical of the pottery of this phase is a red surface slip that has a tendency to flake. Its decoration consists of zig-zag, deeply cut lines often filled with a white paste inlay. The most characteristic shapes are a two-handled chalice on a high conical foot, and a bowl with an axe-shaped handle. At Borġ in-Nadur evidence was met with not only of the use but also of the working of metal.

The last episode of the Maltese Bronze Age, the *Baħrija* phase (c. 900–700 B.C.), occupies the last century or two of that age. It is brought about by the arrival on the island, probably from southern Italy, of a small group of new settlers who managed to occupy a previous *Borġ in-Nadur* settlement site, the naturally defended Qlejgħa promontory at Baħrija. Although the latter is the only known settlement site of this people so far, typical pottery has been found at other excavated sites, such as Għar Dalam, Borġ in-Nadur and Tas-Silġ. This means that the *Baħrija* folk did not isolate themselves from the contemporary *Borġ in-Nadur* inhabitants. The characteristic pottery is dark grey to black with a black slip. The decoration, consisting of geometric patterns, like triangles, zigzags and meanders, is produced by square-sectioned, chiselled grooves normally filled with white paste. Some painted sherds suggest a strong link with the Fossa Grave cultures of Calabria.

A seated terracotta figurine with extremely stylized features and a large fan-like headdress. The female sex is denoted by two small knobs on the chest. From Tarxien Cemetery. H. 0.22m.

A

B

C

D

From Tarxien Cemetery.

A Typical bowl with incised geometric decoration. H. 0.072m.

B Similarly decorated double vase. H. 0.07m.

C Undecorated vase with six spouts. A multi-wicked oil-lamp? H. 0.15m.

D Copper axe-heads and dagger-blades.

Two-handled chalice. A typical shape of the *Borġ in-Nadur* phase complete examples of which have been found at Thapsos and Ognina in Sicily. H. 0.22m.

A beautiful bowl of the *Baħrija* phase with an elaborate geometric decoration: incised and filled with white paste against a dark black, polished background. H. 0.065m.

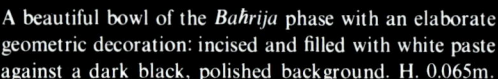

Section of the Bronze Age rampart protecting the *Borġ in-Nadur* settlement.

One of two dolmens on the right of the road from Mosta to Għargħur (Fuq Wied il-Għasel).

Aerial views of the Gozo Citadel and Mdina, Malta. Underneath these and the adjacent towns of Rabat lie the ancient towns of *Gaudos* and *Melite*.

ANCIENT HISTORY

THE FIRST LITERATE PEOPLE: THE PHOENICIANS

The beginning of history in Malta around 700 B.C. is not marked, as one would normally expect, by a written document, a literary allusion or an inscription. It is a somewhat conventional landmark based on the earliest available evidence of a literate people, the Phoenicians, present on the islands certainly about that date, probably even before. This evidence consists of typically western Phoenician pottery items found in a tomb at Għajn Qajjet, near Rabat, which could be dated with greater precision by means of two closely datable Greek imports: a Protocorinthian cup (first half of the 7th century B.C.) and a Rhodian 'bird' bowl (second half of the 7th century B.C.). So far other tombs belonging to this early period (i.e. 700–550 B.C.) have turned up only in the neighbourhood of Rabat (Malta) and Rabat (Gozo). One is thus led to assume that both the Rabat-Mdina promontory and the Rabat-Citadel hill were already on the way to becoming the chief urban settlements of the two islands, as we know they were in Roman times.

Phoenician artefacts of the archaic period have, however, been discovered on another important site that was excavated in the 1960s by Italian archaeologists: the Tas-Silġ sanctuary overlooking the Marsaxlokk harbour on the southeast coast. Here, we are told, these Phoenician remains were found not only in layers immediately overlying others representing the Bronze Age prehistoric cultures but also, in some cases, mixed with *Borġ in-Nadur* pottery. This constitutes the first available evidence of a coexistence between the Phoenician new comers and the prehistoric people they found already established on the two islands. On the other hand we are still curious to know the size and consistency of the Phoenician presence in Malta. Was Malta only a convenient port of call on the long stretch of open sea between Phoenicia and Carthage? Did they establish a small emporium on the islands with only a few Phoenician families looking after the needs of the calling Phoenician ships, a sort of shipping agency? Or was a fully fledged Phoenician colony planted there? In the latter case when did it happen? Unfortunately these questions have to remain without an answer for the present. But one hopes that there are still undestroyed sources of evidence to be tapped by the archaeologist under the Maltese soil.

Gilt ornamental ivory fragment in open work. Half of an orientalizing voluted capital with hanging palmette. From Tas-Silġ. H. 0.076m. 7th–6th century B.C.

Among the objects retrieved from these tombs, which testify both inhumation and cremation rites, one cannot fail to mention the bronze torch-holder, of Cypro-Phoenician type, from the same tomb of Għajn Qajjet, the items of silver jewelry from the tomb at Rabat, Gozo, and the gold jewelry from a tomb at Għajn Klieb.

The only architectural structure that has been attributed to this period is the sanctuary dedicated to the Phoenician goddess Astarte at Tas-Silġ which incorporated the megalithic temple mentioned above. Apart from the archaic pottery found there, perhaps the most notable non-architectural object is a finely carved, gilt ivory fragment preserving the right half of a stylized capital with an elaborate palmette hanging from the volute.

Archaic Greek pottery items from tombs near Rabat.

A   Proto-Corinthian cup (*skyphos*) from Mtarfa. H. 0.084m. Early 7th century B.C.

B   Corinthian *kotyle* from Mtarfa. H. 0.14m. End of 7th-beginning of 6th century B.C.

C. Eastern Greek 'bird-bowl' from Għajn Qajjet. H. 0.055m. Second half of 7th century B.C.

THEIR SUCCESSORS: THE CARTHAGINIANS

As the political autonomy of the Phoenician cities in the motherland gradually declined at the hands of the powerful empires that succeeded each other in the east, the colonies in the west became increasingly independent. One of these, Carthage, grew so prosperous and powerful that it actually set up new colonies of its own and eventually assumed the hegemony of the western colonies and championed them whenever they clashed with the other powers in the region: the Greek cities of Sicily first, and later the Romans. It is in the light of these developments that the period from the middle of the 6th century onwards is labelled the 'Punic' (or 'Carthaginian') period.

Although politically and militarily Malta must have depended heavily on Carthage, as can be surmised from the recorded events towards the end of this period, its commercial and cultural ties were by far stronger with the Greek cities of Sicily and Magna Grecia and with Punic Tripolitania. South Italian black-glazed and red-figured pottery is relatively common and the tomb furniture of the 4th-3rd centuries B.C. is closely paralleled in the necropolis of Leptis.

Rock-cut tombs of the Phoenician type become much more widely spread and are often encountered in various parts of Malta, though they are surprisingly scarce in Gozo. Close to Rabat-Mdina they assume the character of entire necropoleis (town cemeteries). One such tomb at Għar Barka produced the anthropomorphic terracotta sarcophagus now in the National Museum of Archaeology in Valletta. Another tomb at Tal-Virtù contained an Egyptianizing bronze pendant which in its cavity carried a tiny piece of papyrus. On the latter is a prayer for protection from evil superimposed on a figure of the Egyptian goddess Isis.

Away from the main town, the sanctuary of Tas-Silġ continued to flourish and between the 4th and 1st centuries B.C. it was extensively restructured with the addition of monumental gateways, porticoes and pavings of stone slabs or *opus signinum*. In the opposite direction a new sanctuary appeared on the Ras il-Wardija promontory in Gozo. It was partly built and partly rock-cut and lasted only a couple of centuries. The only other known structure belonging to this period is the square building in Zurrieq crowned by a cornice of Egyptian inspiration and Phoenician typology. It has survived remarkably well but archaeological investigations to ascertain its purpose and

Bronze amulet from a tomb at Tal-Virtù, Rabat. It contained a tiny papyrus scroll with a Phoenician inscription superimposed on a drawing of Isis. H. 0.048m. 6th century B.C.

date have proved fruitless. The round towers a few of which survive in the fast disappearing Maltese countryside may also belong to this period and may have formed part of a defence system. Lastly it seems that some of the Roman rustic villas had predecessors during this period, as is borne out by evidence from the villas of San Pawl Milqi, Ta' Kaċċatura, and Żejtun.

Terracotta anthropomorphic sarcophagus from a tomb at Għar Barka, Rabat. L. 1.55m. 5th century B.C.

Small Punic amphora of a type most probably of Maltese production and exported to other Mediterranean centres. H. c.0.30m.

One of a pair of marble candelabra with bilingual inscriptions in Greek and Punic. Dedications to Herakles/Melqart. Its companion is in the Louvre. Max. H. 1.05m. 2nd century B.C.

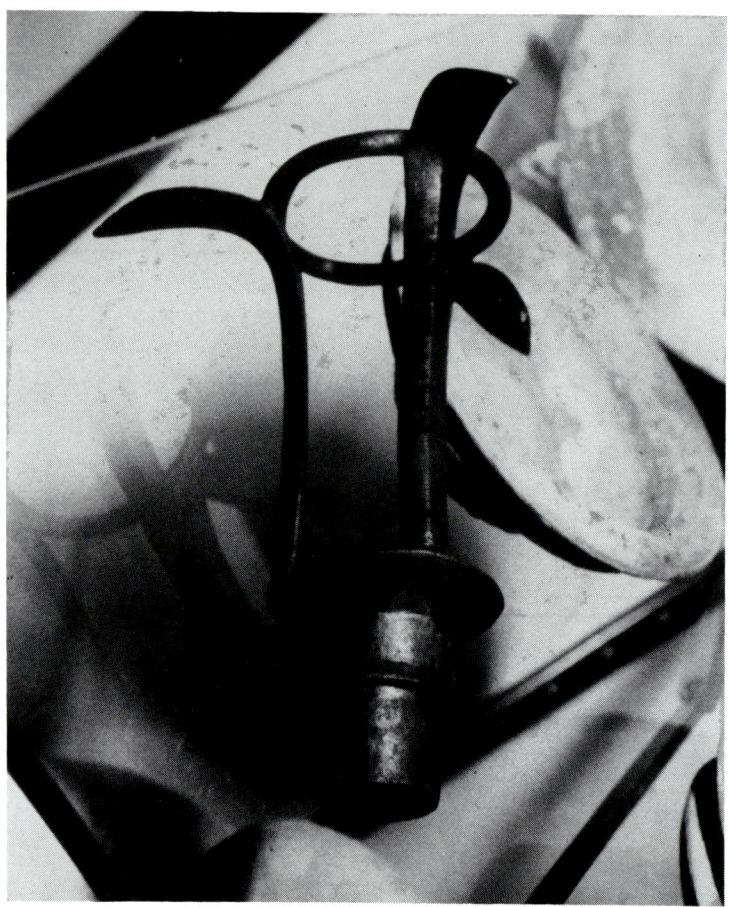

Bronze torch-holder of Cypro-Phoenician origin. From tomb at Għajn Qajjet. H. 0.14m. 7th century B.C.

Cathedral Museum, Mdina. Two Carthaginian coins, one gold and the other bronze, in circulation in many Punic centres, including Malta. Obverse: female divinity (Persephone or Tanit). Reverse: free horse.

Small square structure, probably part of destroyed Punic building, with characteristic Egyptianizing cornice. Żurrieq, private garden. Note the perfect fit and size of the masonry (c. 0.66 × 1.80m.) compared with that of the modern wall attached to it.

THE GREAT IMPERIALISTS: THE ROMANS

It was almost by accident that Malta was incorporated in the Roman commonwealth in 218 B.C. But it was an inevitable fate. By that year, which marks the beginning of the Second Punic war – known also as the Hannibalic war – Rome had conquered the whole of the Italian peninsula, Sardinia and most of Sicily. The consul Ti. Sempronius Longus sailed from Lilybaeum to Malta in search of the Carthaginian fleet. He did not find it there but invaded the island instead with the intention of securing the southern flank. The island together with the Carthaginian garrison capitulated without resistance. With the end of the second Punic war Malta and Gozo started to form part of the province of Sicily. From then on the archipelago was destined to share for centuries the same fate with the larger island.

The Punic culture, in spite of gradual Roman acculturation, survived for centuries under Roman domination. The survival of the language during the first two centuries is attested by the Punic legends on the coins minted in Malta and by several inscriptions datable to the 2nd and 1st centuries B.C. Its tenacity among the lower social categories is borne out indirectly by the narrator of the episode of St. Paul's shipwreck on the island in the Acts of the Apostles. He labelled 'barbaroi' the country people who came to the rescue of the shipwrecked, meaning that they were not familiar with either Greek or Latin. The Punic funerary tradition, using underground rock-cut chambers in single or double units, continued until the very end of the Roman period when the Palaeochristian tradition took over and expanded many of them into extensive and interconnected catacombs. Even Punic religion was allowed to be practised alongside the Roman official cults.

The Romanization of the islands coincided with the intensification of another cultural component, the Greek one, which had already started to permeate the Semitic culture of the Punic inhabitants of the western Mediterranean, including those of Malta and Carthage itself. The stronger impact of Greek culture on the way of life of the Maltese in the Roman period is certainly due to increased contact with the Greek population of Sicily as a result of the new political and administrative arrangement. This influence can be gleaned from inscriptions, in the Greek legends and the Hellenized iconography on some of the locally struck coins, as well as in the pair of identical marble candelabra, probably of Hellenistic production but carrying dedications in both Greek and Punic.

By Roman times, if not before, Malta had a major urban centre, the town of *Melite* (Rabat-Mdina), as is testified by the famous orator and lawyer M. Tullius Cicero in his prosecution speeches against the former governor of Sicily and Malta, Caius Verres. In the 2nd century A.D. the geographer Ptolemy mentions a town for Gozo (*Gaudos*) along with that of *Melite*. Various relics of Roman buildings have been met with in the past while digging in Rabat and Mdina. Some architectural features (columns, capitals, cornices) still survive and are preserved in the Museum of Roman Antiquities in Rabat. In the same museum one can also see an inscription discovered in 1774 inside Mdina which describes various details of a temple dedicated to Apollo. Religious and public buildings are also suggested for the town of *Gaudos* by several inscriptions and architectural fragments. The most spectacular Roman building ever to be uncovered in either of the islands is the Roman town house of Rabat, just outside the Mdina fortifications. It must have belonged to a rich dignitary. The structure itself is dated by the architecture and by the mosaics to the first half of the 1st century B.C. Its main feature is the peristyle in the Doric order that surrounded a courtyard paved with an attractive mosaic. Around the peristyle were a series of rooms, one of which seems to be the dining room, the *triclinium*. Both peristyle and surrounding rooms were decorated with floor mosaics which have survived in fragments. In the majority of cases they consisted of geometric designs (some with complicated optical effects) with centrally placed *emblemata* (small square scenes in *opus vermiculatum*).

In the first century A.D., moreover, the occupier of the house made sure to embellish it by a series of imported marble statues, some carrying the portraits of members of the Imperial family. In fact, besides a number of togate statues and draped female torsos, all headless, two magnificent portraits were retrieved during the excavations of 1881, one representing the emperor Claudius (A.D. 41–54) and the other his mother Antonia the Younger. These two portraits rank among the finest specimens of Roman portraiture.

Beside the two main towns the Maltese population of the Roman period must have inhabited also other small centres, most probably in the areas close to the harbours. For these, however, the only evidence consists of relative concentrations of tombs, such as in the Salina area and in the Żejtun–Paola–Marsa area. On the other hand, we know of about 25 villas scattered on the islands' countryside only a few of which seem to have been of the purely residential type, the rest corresponding more to modern farmsteads attached to large country estates. The latter, besides a section of the building destined for habitation, had an area intended for agricultural activities, the most evident of which is the processing of olive oil.

The sanctuary of Tas-Silġ was still flourishing in this period as is testified by archaeological findings. It is almost certainly the sanctuary of the goddess Juno extolled as world-famous by the orator Cicero and singled out as an important landmark by Ptolemy in his *Geography*. Ptolemy mentions another temple in Malta, dedicated to Hercules, which has not yet been securely identified. Towards the end of the 5th century A.D. a new building was erected at Tas-Silġ, a Palaeochristian church, thus opening a new chapter in the cultural and religious history of the Maltese people. The vast number of tombs, collective hypogea and catacombs, of a recognizable Christian typology, dispersed all over the island, but with a much greater concentration just outside *Melite*, suggest that by the 6th century the majority of the Maltese population was Christian. A number of small hypogea of a clearly Jewish typology reveal, however, the co-existence of a small Jewish community.

The end of the Roman period in Malta is placed by some at the end of the 4th century (A.D. 395), that is the Theodosian division of the Empire. But the first clear literary evidence that the islands were incorporated in the Byzantine Empire dates to the second quarter of the 6th century, that is when Sicily fell to the Byzantines (A.D. 535).

Mosaic floors at the Roman baths of Għajn Tuffieħa. The *tepidarium* and one of a series of small rooms (changing rooms?). The former was equipped with carved stone benches.

Mosaic pavements from the 'Roman Villa' in Rabat, Malta.

A Detached fragment showing part of a frame decorated with a festoon and a series of theatrical masks in *opus vermiculatum*.

B *Emblema* in the centre of the peristyle showing two doves perched on bronze basin.

C The whole floor of the peristyle courtyard showing a polychrome meander pattern with remarkable optical illusion. Early 1st century B.C.

B

C

'Roman Villa' at Rabat. Parts of one surviving column and a section of the Doric entablature of the peristyle. The left column is a modern copy. Early 1st century B.C.

Museum of Roman Antiquities, Rabat. Marble sculpture found during the excavations of the 'Roman Villa' in 1881.

Portrait bust of Antonia the Younger (36B.C.–A.D.37), mother of emperor Claudius. Max. H. 0.50m.

Lower half of a draped female statue of a type derived from the *kore* of Praxiteles. Max. H. 1.12m. Julio-Claudian: 1st half of 1st century A.D.

Portrait head of emperor Claudius (reigned A.D. 41–54). H. 0.33m.

Section of a huge cistern attached to the Roman Villa at Ta' Kaċċatura near Birżebbuġa. The cistern is hewn out of the rock and roofed over by a system of thick and long stone slabs supported by massive pilasters at regular intervals.

Museum of Roman Antiquities, Rabat. A typical Roman olive mill reconstructed from original stone parts.

Salina Catacombs. A canopied grave with elaborate decoration in relief. A section of the *mensa* is visible in the foreground.

Museum of Roman Antiquities, Rabat. Mouldmade lamp with a deep circular body. The discus is decorated by a rosette in relief surrounding the filling-hole. Crescent-shaped handle. Early 1st century A.D.

THE MALTESE CART RUTS

The enigmatic cart ruts are too obvious in the Maltese rocky landscape to be ignored in any work, however concise, on Maltese archaeology even though they are still not easy to locate in the chronological sequence. According to the traditional view, they should be placed in prehistory, more precisely in the Bronze Age, the main argument being that some specimens are cut by 'Punic' tombs and, therefore, should be prior to that period. The validity of this argument is, in my view, highly questionable particularly since for Temi Zammit, its originator, 'Punic' could mean anything from the 7th century B.C. to the 3rd century A.D., especially as far as tombs are concerned. In my search and study of ancient quarries over the last fifteen years, I found cart ruts very frequently, almost invariably, associated with them. The best example is, perhaps, the Buskett group which lies next to the largest and most important of Malta's ancient quarries. For this reason I cannot refrain from believing that they were intended for the transportation of construction blocks from the quarry face to the road in ancient (i.e., not prehistoric) times. This view is supported by a good number of parallels abroad (for instance in Sicily, southern France and Greece) as well as by their concentration in several areas around *Melite* which must have required a constant supply of ashlar masonry for its buildings.

An example of cart ruts from Naxxar. Two pairs of ruts intersecting each other.